At The Beach

Adaptation of the animated series: Marion Johnson
Illustrations: Eric Sévigny, based on the animated series

It was summer vacation, and Caillou was going to the beach. He couldn't wait to see what the ocean was like.
At last Daddy parked the car. Caillou jumped out and ran down to look at the water.

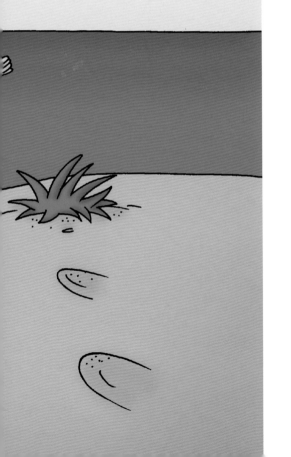

"Wow!" shouted Caillou. "The ocean!"

The ocean went on forever. It was the biggest thing Caillou had ever seen.

"Caillou, it's very sunny, and that means sunscreen," Mommy said.

Caillou giggled and tried to get away, but Mommy held on tight. She covered him all over with sunscreen. It tickled!
When Mommy was finally finished, Caillou ran down the beach.

Daddy set up the umbrella, and Mommy put Rosie down in the shade.

Caillou didn't want to sit in the shade. He wanted to do something!

"Anyone want to go swimming?" Daddy asked.

"Me! Me!" Caillou jumped up and took Daddy's hand. Together they ran into the water.

Brrrr! "The water is cold," Caillou said.

"It's all right once you get used to it," Daddy told him.

Suddenly a big wave knocked Daddy down.

Caillou laughed because Daddy looked funny.

Then a wave knocked Caillou down. Caillou giggled. This was fun!

"Hey, you two." Mommy called.
"Time for lunch."
The two swimmers came out of
the water hungry after fighting
the waves. They dried off and
sat down.
Caillou had a sandwich and
some lemonade for his lunch.
Yummy!

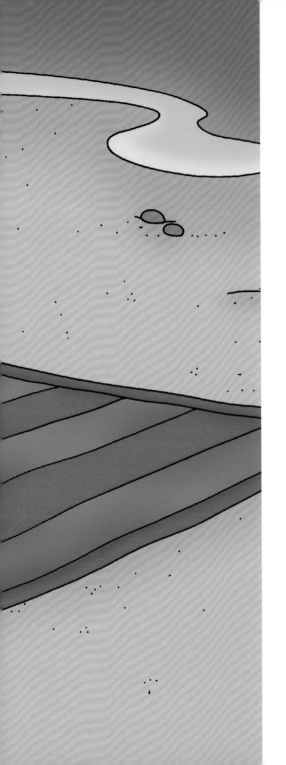

Caillou picked up his sandwich and took a big bite, but now it was full of sand. So he put it down.
A seagull flew by and swooped down to get the sandy sandwich!
"Hey, come back!" exclaimed Caillou. "That's mine!"

After lunch, Caillou went exploring along the beach. He found a little pool of sea water and lay down to take a closer look.
Look at all the kinds of sea creatures swimming in it!

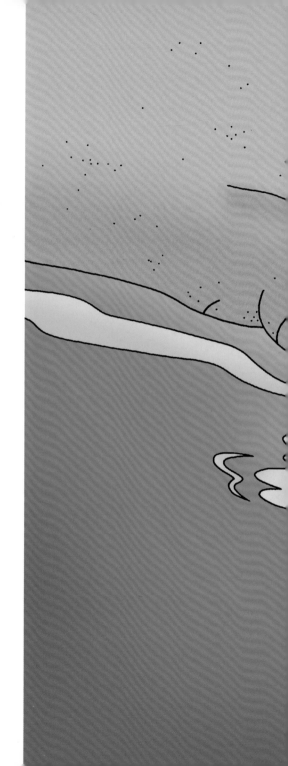

Caillou ran back when he
heard Mommy calling, "Want
to build a sandcastle, Caillou?"
Caillou showed Rosie how
to make towers.
"Look, Rosie," he said. "You
take the pail and go like this."
Rosie giggled and clapped her
hands. Sandcastles were the
most fun of all!

Suddenly Caillou felt water splashing him. The ocean had moved closer, and the castle was washing away!

"What happened?" Caillou asked. "The tide makes the water get higher and lower," Mommy explained. "Right now, the tide is coming in. And that means it's time for us to go."

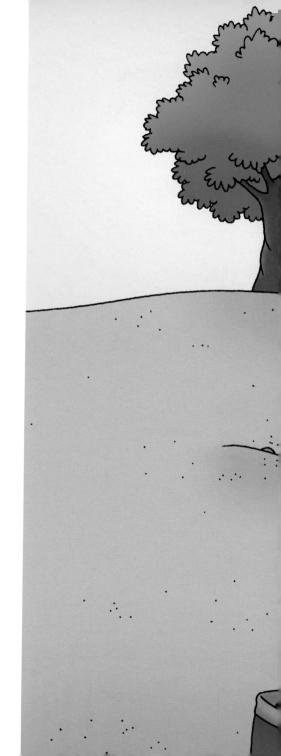

Mommy and Daddy gathered up all their things and headed for the car.

"Don't worry, Caillou," Mommy said. "We can come back tomorrow and build another sandcastle."

Caillou smiled. "I want to come back tomorrow and the next day and the next day. This is the best vacation ever!"

Text: adaptation by Marion Johnson of the animated series CAILLOU,
produced by DHX Media Inc.
All rights reserved.
Original story written by Stephen Ashton.
Illustrations: Eric Sévigny, based on the animated series CAILLOU
Art Direction: Monique Dupras

The PBS KIDS logo is a registered mark of PBS and is used with permission.

We acknowledge the financial support of the Government of Canada through
the Canada Book Fund for our publishing activities.

Canadian Patrimoine
Heritage canadien

We acknowledge the support of the Ministry of Culture and Communications
of Quebec and SODEC for the publication and promotion of this book.

SODEC
Québec

Bibliothèque et Archives nationales du Québec and
Library and Archives Canada cataloguing in publication

Johnson, Marion, 1949-
Caillou at the beach
New ed.
(Clubhouse)
Originally issued in series: Scooter. 2003.
For children aged 3 and up.
ISBN 978-2-89450-942-5

1. Water - Recreational use - Juvenile literature. 2. Beach - Juvenile
literature. I. Sévigny, Éric. II. Title. III. Series: Clubhouse.

GV1218.A68J63 2012   j797.2'5   C2011-942848-2

Printed in Canada
10 9 8 7 6 5 4 3 2   CHO1930 DEC2014